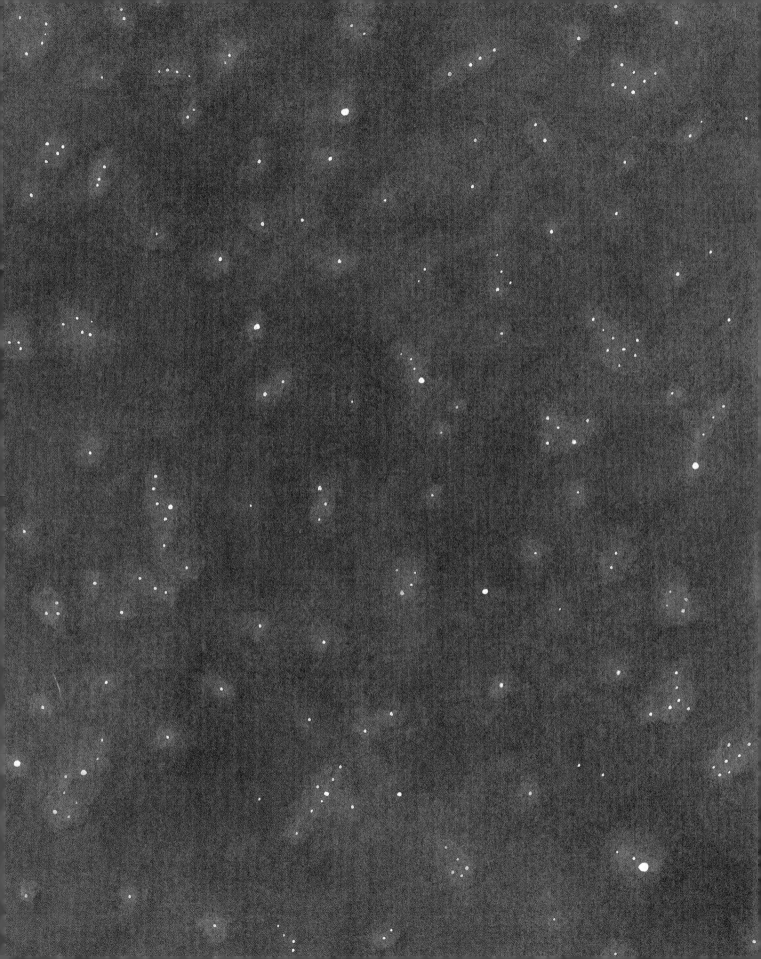

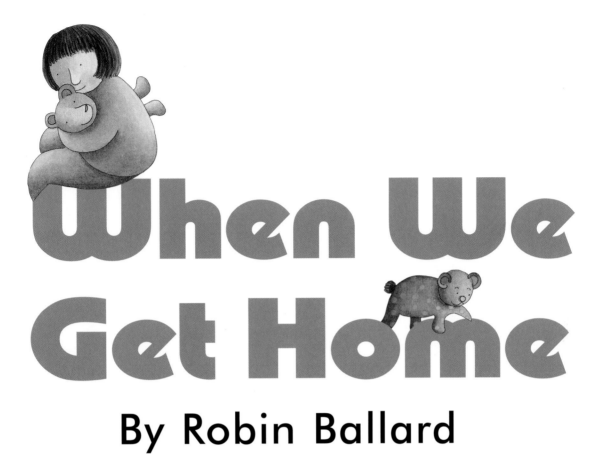

When We Get Home

By Robin Ballard

Greenwillow Books, New York

For Martin and Jasper

Pen and ink and watercolors
were used for the full-color art.
The text type is Futura Bold.

Printed in Hong Kong by South
China Printing Company (1988) Ltd.

First Edition

10 9 8 7 6 5 4 3 2 1

Library of Congress
Cataloging-in-Publication Data

Ballard, Robin.
When we get home / by Robin Ballard.
 p. cm.
Summary: On her way home in the car,
a girl thinks about how she will say
good-night to her family, get ready
for bed, and go to sleep.
ISBN 0-688-16168-5
[1. Bedtime—Fiction.
2. Family life—Fiction.] I. Title.
PZ7.B2125WI 1999 [E]—dc21
98-3446 CIP AC

Today Mama and I helped Granny move. Now it is late and we are on our way home. We drive down the quiet streets. We drive down the empty highways.

The moon is bright in the night sky. It hides in the trees or behind tall buildings. Sometimes it is on my side and sometimes right in back of me. The moon is following me all the way home.

When we get home, the

porch light will be on and

Kitty will want to come

in where it's warm.

Papa will be waiting for us.

We will have to wake him up

because he has fallen asleep

in front of the TV.

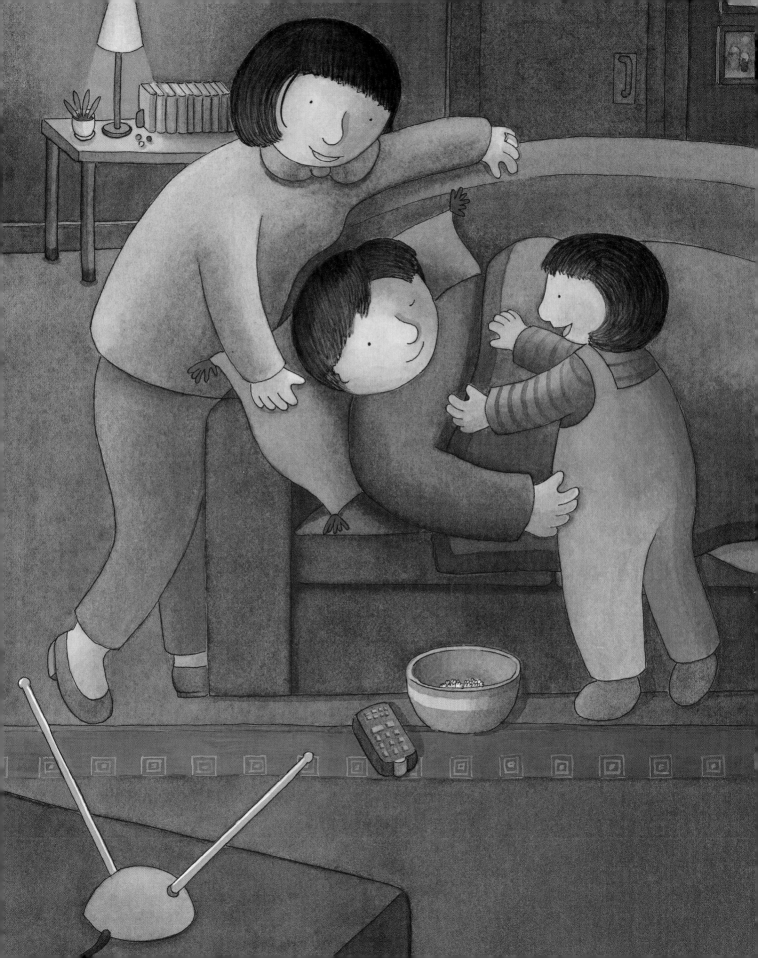

I will go to the bathroom

to brush my teeth

and use the toilet.

I will go to the baby's room and whisper good-night to my sleeping sister. I will go to my room and put on my pajamas.

Mama will close the curtains

and bring me a glass of water,

in case I am thirsty in the night.

Papa will turn off the light.

He will tuck me in under the covers.

There will be no bedtime story

because it is so late.

Both Mama and Papa will

give me a kiss.

"Sleep tight," they will say.

"We'll see you in the morning."

And before I fall asleep,

I will see the moon,

which has followed me

all the way home.

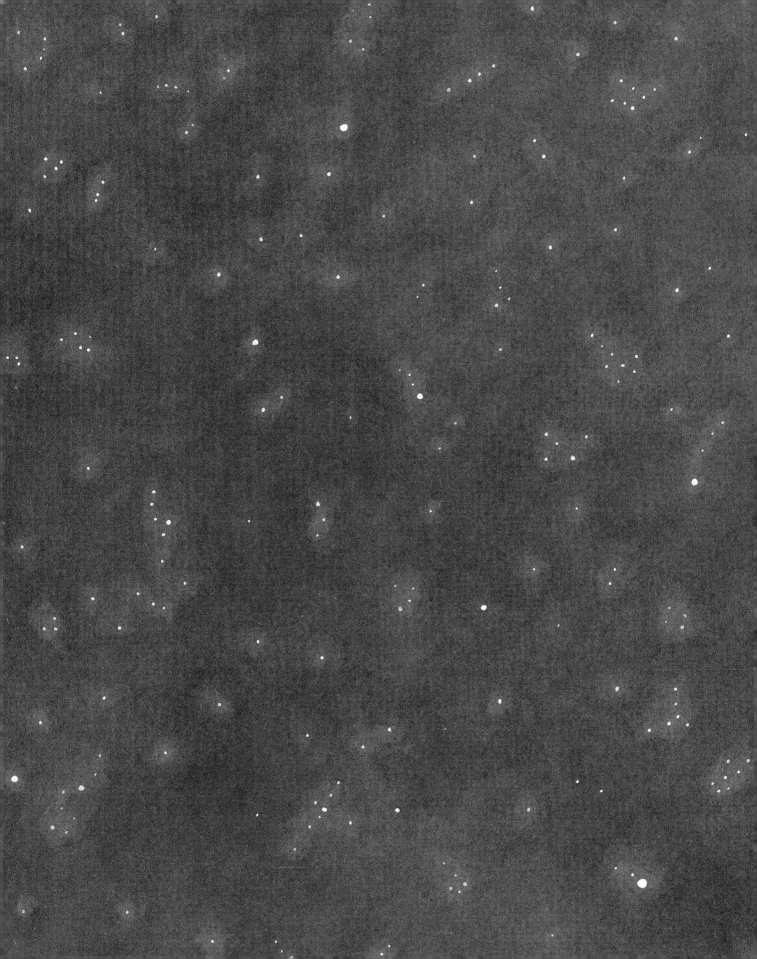